Declan Grows Up
It's Just Not Fair

Written By: C. Austin Lee

Illustrated By: Quinn Feeney Lee

AMERICAN VALUES
PUBLISHING COMPANY

Newport Beach, California

American Values Publishing Company, LLC
P.O. Box 10248
Newport Beach, CA 92658

www.AmericanValuesPublishing.com

Library of Congress Control Number: 2012923304
ISBN - 13: 978-1-939097-00-2 (Hardback)

Printed in the United States of America

In Loving Memory Of:

Cedric Charles Scarlett
"The sky is the limit!"

"A winner is someone who recognizes his God-given talents,
works his tail off to develop them into skills,
and uses these skills to accomplish his goals."
-Larry Bird

"**It's just not fair!**" cried the little lion Declan to his mother. "Today at school we played basketball during gym class and Joey the giraffe blocked every one of my shots."

"He is so much taller than everyone. It is **just not fair!**"

"I tried to shoot the ball from the right side but Joey blocked it. I tried to shoot the ball from the left side and he blocked it. I tried to shoot the ball from the middle and guess what? Joey blocked that one too!" said Declan with frustration in his voice.

"Do you want to know what else Joey did?" asked Declan.

"Joey scored 25 baskets and his team ended up winning the game. I couldn't block any of his shots because he is so tall. I jumped as high as I could over and over again and even climbed up on Julian's shoulders."

"No matter what I did I simply couldn't block any of Joey's shots."

"It's just not fair!"

Declan's voice became louder and he began pacing as he said, "If it wasn't for Joey I am sure I would be the best basketball player on the Great Grassy Plain. I would easily dribble the ball up and down the court. I would block the other team's shots and all of my shots would go in without Joey there to block them."

"They shouldn't let Joey play anymore.
It's just not fair!" Declan cried out.

"Now Declan, let me teach you something that your wise grandpa Cedric taught me many years ago," said Declan's mother.

"When I was a little girl I wanted to learn to dance like the monkeys. They were so graceful and funny."

"I used to watch them dance on their hind legs. Jump here, jump there, jump everywhere and swing from branch to branch and tree to tree."

"I tried so hard to be like the monkeys. I jumped from here to there. I tried to dance on my hind legs. I even tried to jump from tree to tree," explained Declan's mother.

"What happened?" asked Declan.

I fell from the tree and hurt my head. Your grandfather picked
me up and asked what I was doing. I cried, "I have tried and
tried, but I can't dance like the monkeys. It's just not fair!"

"What did grandpa say?" asked Declan.

He told me that life is not always fair and that everyone is born with different gifts, abilities and talents.

"What do you mean?" asked Declan.

Declan's mother said, "Joey was born with gifts including his height that help him play basketball well. The monkeys were born with gifts that allow them to dance, and I was born with abilities that allow me to be your mother."

"Well I wish I was born with gifts that would allow me to play basketball like Joey," exclaimed Declan.

"And I am sure Joey wishes he had some of your talents," replied Declan's mother. "In fact, I bet there are many others who wish they had your abilities and talents too."

"What are my abilities and talents?" asked Declan.

"I am glad you asked," said Declan's mother. "You have tried so many different things. You have played soccer and basketball. You are taking trumpet lessons. You are learning many new things in school. I even heard you singing in the shower yesterday. What do you think you are good at and what do you like to do?"

"I really like soccer, even more than basketball and I play well most days," replied Declan with excitement in his voice.
"I am getting better at the trumpet but it isn't my favorite. I like school and enjoy learning new things."

"Did you really hear me singing?" asked Declan with an embarrassed look on his face.

"I did hear you and can tell you now that singing isn't one of your gifts," said his mother laughing.

"So what do you think my gifts are?" asked Declan.

"It seems like you have abilities that allow you to do well in soccer and school. If you work hard in soccer practice and work hard in school your talents and skills will grow, just like you grow every year," replied Declan's mother.

"What could I do with my gifts and abilities?" asked Declan.

"There are many things you can do with them," responded his mother. "You could become a professional soccer player or a soccer coach if you grow your gifts in soccer."

"You could become almost anything: a policeman, a teacher, a pilot, a doctor or even the King of the Jungle if you grow your skills and abilities in school!"

"So what should I do?" asked Declan.

"Spend your life trying new things so you can discover all the gifts, talents and abilities you were born with. Spend every day practicing them and growing them. Find people who can help you grow your gifts. Use your talents to make your life better and to help others," explained his mother.

Learn that life is not fair. We don't always get the gifts we want. Instead of feeling bad and sad, ask yourself, "What am I good at?" and "What do I like to do?"

Declan spent the rest of the year working on his talents that allow him to do well in soccer and school, and he tried many new things. He won his class spelling bee, solved a puzzle that no one else in his class could and is excited for the first game of the upcoming soccer season.

What do you think your gifts, talents and abilities are?

What are you good at? What do you like to do?

Lesson Discussion Guide:

This story illustrates the lesson that life is not fair. Each of us is born into a different set of circumstances with different gifts, skills and abilities. We don't always get the gifts we wish we had, like the physical and innate abilities that would allow us to excel at a professional sport. However, for every gift, skill or ability we wish we had, there are countless others that wish they had what we have.

Some dream of being able to dunk a basketball while others dream of being able to walk. The secret to life is learning what our gifts, skills and abilities are, learning how to use them, and working to improve and perfect them. No one who is good at anything has gotten there without hours upon hours of practicing and perfecting their gifts whether a professional athlete, a concert pianist, a medical doctor, a hairdresser, a business man or woman, or anything for which we have a talent. One of the saddest things in life is to see talent go unrecognized, underutilized or wasted.

Use this story to get your children to begin thinking about their gifts. Have regular conversations with them about their talents, skills and abilities. Expose them to as much as you can by enrolling them in different activities, trying new things, taking them to visit new places, doing research on the internet, etc. If they express an interest in something or seem to have a natural ability in an area, add fuel to their passion. Buy them books about the activity, read articles from experts, connect them with coaches and mentors who can help them develop their skills and abilities and stress the importance of practice. Even if your child loses interest over time the exposure will make them a more rounded person and it is important that they learn the process of recognizing skills and abilities and working to develop them.

By learning to recognize and build upon skills and abilities, you and your children will begin to see that even though life may not be fair, everyone can find a way to prosper and enjoy a rich and fulfilling life.

For more more information please visit **www.AmericanValuesPublishing.com.**

What Are You Good At?

_____

_____

_____

_____

_____

_____

_____

What Do You Like To Do?

_____

_____

_____

_____

_____

_____

_____

_____

_____

About The Author

C. Austin Lee grew up outside Philadelphia, earned a BS in Biology and Business Administration from Muhlenberg College in Allentown, PA and moved to New York City where he earned a MBA from Pace University and advanced through positions of increasing responsibility in sales, marketing, management and business strategy in the Biotech and Medical Device Industries.

Austin was fortunate to have had strong parents, teachers, mentors and coaches to guide him throughout his life and has always tried to do the same for others. He has had the privilege of working with excellent organizations such as the Boy Scouts of America, his church, the West End Youth Center (as a wrestling coach), Big Brothers Big Sisters, and the Westchester Children's Association.

Austin developed the Declan the Lion Series and the American Values Publishing Company, Inc. to help children build a strong foundation of self-esteem and values that will allow them to achieve success in their lives.

C. Austin Lee currently resides in Newport Beach, California with his wife Nicole and dogs Bentley and Calvin. He is the oldest of 17 grandchildren and enjoys spending time with his family including his Aunt Quinn, the illustrator and his nephew and Godson, Declan.

About The Illustrator

Quinn Feeney Lee grew up in Allentown, Pennsylvania. She received her Bachelor of Arts degree at Bloomsburg University. Quinn lives in Montgomeryville, PA with her husband, Bob and her children Michael, Julia, Austin and Mary Kate and dog, Charlie. She loves drawing and painting, but is most passionate about raising her four, wonderful children. Quinn enjoys spending time with her large, extended family including her nephew, author C. Austin Lee.

To learn more about the Declan Grows Up Series and the American Values Publishing Company, please visit us at: www.AmericanValuesPublishing.com

Coming Soon: Declan Grows Up: What Winners Do